KITEBOARDING

Betsy R. Cassriel

Rourke
Educational Media

rourkeeducationalmedia.com

Scan for Related Titles
and Teacher Resources

Before Reading:

Building Academic Vocabulary and Background Knowledge

Before reading a book, it is important to tap into what your child or students already know about the topic. This will help them develop their vocabulary, increase their reading comprehension, and make connections across the curriculum.

1. Look at the cover of the book. What will this book be about?
2. What do you already know about the topic?
3. Let's study the Table of Contents. What will you learn about in the book's chapters?
4. What would you like to learn about this topic? Do you think you might learn about it from this book? Why or why not?
5. Use a reading journal to write about your knowledge of this topic. Record what you already know about the topic and what you hope to learn about the topic.
6. Read the book.
7. In your reading journal, record what you learned about the topic and your response to the book.
8. After reading the book complete the activities below.

Content Area Vocabulary
Read the list. What do these words mean?

acrobatics
aerial
bindings
board shaper
catamarans
gale-force
GPS
harness
intense
knots
rooster tail
starboard
whitecaps
wind window

After Reading:

Comprehension and Extension Activity

After reading the book, work on the following questions with your child or students in order to check their level of reading comprehension and content mastery.

1. What other sports is kiteboarding like? Explain. (Summarize)
2. What are some dangers kiteboarders could encounter? (Asking questions)
3. Can you connect this sport with something else in your life? Share with us. (Text to self connection)
4. Explain why steady wind, not gusty wind, is best for kiteboarding? (Infer)
5. Why do kiteboards have a variety of sizes and styles of kites? (Asking questions)

Extension Activity

Like any sport, kiteboarding has the perfect spots to go to. Use the text and choose one of the many areas professionals go to kiteboard. Research that city and find out why kiteboarding is best there. What other famous attractions and sports are located in that city? Pretend you are an organizer for a PKRA competition in the city you selected. Create a welcome brochure for the professionals highlighting things to do, important places, and the history of the city.

TABLE OF CONTENTS

WHAT A RUSH! 4

GETTING STARTED 6

SPORTS SKILLS 16

GEAR UP 26

THE STARS 32

TO VICTORY! 42

GLOSSARY 46

INDEX 47

SHOW WHAT YOU KNOW 47

WEBSITES TO VISIT 47

ABOUT THE AUTHOR 48

WHAT A RUSH!

Kevin Langeree flew across the surface of the water. Cold spray hit his face. **Whitecaps** bounced across the ocean. The wind was blowing at a perfect 30 **knots** (34 miles per hour). He adjusted the kite that flew high above him for speed. With a huge smile on his face, Kevin yelled, "This is awesome!"

Kevin came from the Netherlands to compete. He was ready to win! He scanned the blue sky above Cape Town, South Africa, for his competitors. On shore, the kiteboarding championship judges calculated how high and how far each rider jumped. They also judged the riders on their tricks at incredible heights.

It was Kevin's turn. With his best trick in mind, he jumped into the air, going for the title of Red Bull King of the Air.

GETTING STARTED

Speed, high jumps, and big waves! Some people say that kiteboarding is the most thrilling sport in the world. Kiting, as it is also called, is a combination of other sports such as surfing, skateboarding, windsurfing, paragliding,

Kiteboarders speed over the water pulled by the power of the wind.

wakeboarding, and snowboarding. Kiteboarding is an **intense** sport of its own, and people all over the world are participating in this popularwater sport.

The website InMotion Kitesurfing says, "Kitesurfing is hands down one of the most insane sports on this planet! We've tried many extreme sports…and this is honestly the one we would choose to do every single day."

Two Sports

What's the difference between kiteboarding and windsurfing? Windsurfers, below, use a sail attached to a board. Kiteboarders use a kite that soars in the air above them.

Kiteboarding or Kitesurfing?

Kiteboarding and kitesurfing are different names for the same sport. Kiteboarding is usually used in the United States and kitesurfing is used in other countries. They both describe using a kite to pull the rider along on a board.

How old do you have to be to try kiteboarding? Kids can start kiteboarding in the water when they are about 12 years old. Even younger kids can practice controlling a kite on the beach. You don't have to be really strong or fit to start, but you have to know how to swim. You must take lessons to learn to kiteboard. It's not the kind of sport you can teach yourself. It is a great way to exercise, enjoy nature, and have a lot of fun!

To start the ride, a kiteboarder, or kiter, straps into a **harness**. The harness is attached to a bar, and from the bar, lines are connected to an inflatable kite. The kiter launches the kite up into the air. Then the kiter walks into shallow water and steps onto the board. The board takes off immediately along the water's surface. It uses the power of the wind to pull the rider forward.

A kiteboarder wears a harness attached to ropes to control the kite.

The Wright brothers practice with kites at Kitty Hawk, North Carolina, in 1902.

KITE POWER: NOT SO NEW

The sport of kiteboarding is new, but using kites for getting around isn't. Check out how kites were used in the past!

- Chinese people used kites thousands of years ago. They made kites from silk, paper, and bamboo.
- Marco Polo brought the first stories of kites to Europe in the 13th century.
- In the 1800s, George Pocock used kites to pull carts on land and boats across water.
- The Wright brothers used kites while developing their airplane in the early 1900s.
- In 1903, Samuel Cody made "man-lifting kites," or power kites. Cody crossed the English Channel in a small boat pulled by a kite. That is 150 miles (241 kilometers)!
- 1860 to 1910 is known as the "golden age of kiting" in Europe. Kites were used to study meteorology, wireless communications, and photography.

A Green Trip

In 2008, a cargo ship left Germany using a huge towing kite 191 square yard towing kite (160 square meters) for its trip across the Atlantic Ocean to Venezuela. The kite saved 20 percent of the ship engine's power!

For hundreds of years people have experimented with wind power and kites. However, the history of using kites and boards as a sport is new. In the 1980s, Dominique and Bruno Legaignoux from France tested the power of kites for pulling all kinds of things. They tried pulling **catamarans**, small fishing boats, water skis, and windsurf boards. They even tested skateboards, inline skates, inflatable boats, and kayaks!

Meanwhile, in the US, other people were experimenting with using kites on the water. Courageous kiters experimented with kites, wind, and waves in Maui in the Hawaiian Islands. In Oregon, Cory Roeseler and his dad, who was an airplane

The first thing a kiteboarder does is make sure there's a good wind.

Kiteboarders can ride waves and whitewater like surfers.

designer, first used waterskis with kites.

In the 1990s, the first kiteboarding competition took place in Maui. The kites were simple, powerful, and dangerous. The experiments continued as everyone looked for the best ways to pull a rider on the water.

Kiteboarding Fun

- **You can just ride across the water, carve waves, or work on jumps and tricks.**

- **You can enjoy the outdoors and beautiful scenery.**

- **The kite and board are lightweight.**

- **You can ride in light or strong winds, flat water, or waves.**

By 1994, the Legaignoux brothers and Cory Roeseler had developed much better kiteboarding equipment. They started companies to sell it. Good equipment became more available to people who loved water sports. Then the Legaignoux brothers produced a bow kite. It was easier on the rider's arms to fly and more stable. The bow kite was great for both beginners and advanced riders. Soon, kiteboarding was the world's fastest-growing water sport.

As kiteboarding equipment improved, professional kiters focused on the cutting edge of style and skill. Then, in 2007 and 2008, some of the pros started to experiment with extreme weather conditions. They kiteboarded in **gale-force** winds. They wanted to see how high and how far they could go. Today there are many different styles of kiting, from recreational to extreme.

Pulled by strong wind, kiteboarders can fly above the water to do tricks.

SPORTS SKILLS

Kiteboarding is an intense sport. It can be dangerous. The big kite used for kiteboarding is very powerful. Kite skills are the most important part of learning to kitesurf.

A kiteboarder uses the wind like a sailor. Being able to fly the kite without looking at it is very important. You need steady, not gusty, wind. The best wind for most people is between 12 and 20 miles (19.3 and 32 kilometers) per hour, but a pro can fly a kiteboard in 40 mile (64 kilometer) per hour winds!

Beginning kiteboarders often need help getting their kites ready to fly.

Kiters practice their sport all around the world in oceans, lakes, bays, and rivers. Wave conditions are important to consider. New riders should learn to kiteboard when the waves are knee high or smaller. A more advanced kiteboarder can ride larger waves. Experienced kiters like to surf the waves and use them as ramps to jump into the air.

No Water? No Problem!

Don't live near water? Try kiting with a mountainboard, called kite-landboarding, or with a snowboard or skis, called snow-kiting.

Before he hits the water, this kiteboarder is testing the wind and determining its direction.

Before you begin to kiteboard, you have to learn how to keep yourself, the kite, and other beachgoers safe. You need to learn these basics:

- safety rules and regulations on and off the water
- weather conditions and how the **wind window** works
- how to set up your kite correctly
- how to launch, land, and fly the kite safely

If you are a beginner, kitesurf away from crowds and boats so you do not hurt yourself and others. The lines on the kite can be from 65 to 131 feet (20 to 40 meters) long. That is about as long as an NBA basketball court or almost three school buses! Because of this, a beginner who is learning to control the kite has to fly it away from others.

A good way to start kiteboarding is to learn to launch right from the beach.

Have you ever flown a kite? Did your kite ever lose the wind and fall out of the sky? Just like flying a kite in the park, kiteboarders have to keep their kites in the wind to fly. If they don't, their kites will fall into the water. That's where the wind window comes in.

When the wind is blowing at your back, the wind window is everything you can see from ground to sky. You can think of the wind window like a clock. When the kite is directly overhead, it is at 12 o'clock.

The wind window is important to understand for kiteboarding. Using the wind window lets kiteboarders manage the power of the kite. It also helps them go where they want to go.

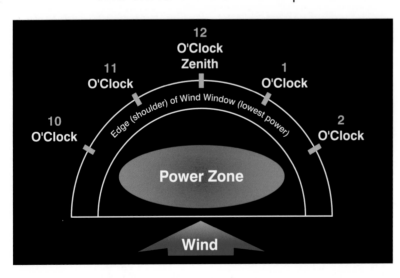

The wind window is a kiteboarder's guide for riding.

At busy beaches on windy days, the sky can be filled with soaring kites.

With the kite directly overhead, kiteboarders can use the Power Zone to create speed.

There are three zones in the wind window. When the kite is directly overhead, at 12 o'clock, this is the Power Zone. Kiteboarders use the Power Zone to get maximum speed for a water start or **aerial** tricks.

Everything between 9 and 12 or 12 and 3 has medium power. This zone is best when the wind strength is good and the rider wants to simply cruise. At 9 o'clock or 3 o'clock, the zone is called the Edge. The Edge has the least power. Kiters use the Edge for launching and landing the kite on the beach. They also use this zone to rest the kite in the water if needed.

When the kite is flying, it tends to move downward to the Edge. Kiters have to pull, or swoop, the kite to get it higher again. A deep, fast swoop can give a lot of power!

Moving the kite to the Edge lets the rider make turns or slow down.

How do you make the kite pull you in a certain direction? Kiteboarders only use half the wind window at a time. The half they use depends on what direction they want to go. To go to the right, or **starboard**, kiteboarders put their kites between 12 and 3 o'clock. They do the opposite to go left, also called port. As they move the sail, they turn the board in the direction they want to move as well.

This kiteboarder churns up the water as he pulls hard into a turn.

Kiteboarders make turns by moving the board with their feet and pulling the kite to one side or the other.

GEAR UP

Kiters need good equipment. Various kite sizes and line lengths are used for different purposes. For starting out, a trainer kite is best. These kites are very small. They are safe for beginners because they do not use as much power as a bigger kite. They are easy to launch, too.

An average rider's kite is 30 to 40 feet (10 to 12 meters) long. That is as long as a school bus! Most kites have four

The lines of a kite usually attach to the four corners.

or five lines. The lines are attached to the control bar. The rider holds the control bar. By pulling at the ends of the bar, the rider rotates the kite in the wind window.

Many kiteboarders

Here's a close up look at the harness, control bar, and lines used to guide the kite.

have several kites. They call their collection of kites a quiver. They choose a kite depending on the weather conditions. Kiteboarders usually choose from four types of kites: C Kites, bow kites, hybrid kites, and Delta kites.

Talkin' Kiteboarding

Here are the names of some of the tricks experts can do:

Canadian Bacon: A rider grabs the board with the rear hand on the toeside, between the feet and through the legs.

Invert: a rider goes Upside down while in the air.

Kiteloop: a rider Loops the kite while in the air.

Stomp: a rider Stomps a trick when they land it in a smooth or clean manner.

Kiteboards come in several shapes and sizes. They match the rider's skill level and riding style, as well as wind and water conditions. For example, beginners use a large, flat board. A smaller board is better if a more experienced rider is flying in higher winds and wants to do jumps. In lighter winds, a longer board is often better.

Kiteboarders choose boards depending on their style of riding, too. Some boards are like surfboards for kiters

Footstraps keep the rider and board together.

The small fins on the kiteboard help the rider to steer the board.

who like to ride waves. Race kiteboards
are made to go fast. They are large boards
with two long fins and foot straps. Many
boards are designed for freestyling. These
boards are the most technical. They have
two edges and are smaller. They turn easily.
Wakestyle boards are very sturdy, and have
channels and small fins. These boards are
especially made for doing tricks with ramps
closer to the water.

The kiteboarder's body actually takes most of the pull of the kite, leaving the arms free to steer.

Kiteboarders wear a harness that connects them to the control bar. This harness takes the stress off the rider's arms. This bar also has a safety release system. If kite lines get tangled or snagged on something, it can be very dangerous for the rider. If the safety release system doesn't work, kiteboarders can use a safety knife. This knife is required equipment for kiteboarding.

Some kiters use a wetsuit, booties, lifejacket, helmet, and sunglasses. They can also carry wind meters, GoPro cameras, and a **GPS**. The meters help measure wind speed. The cameras can produce awesome video. The GPS helps them find their way if they get lost.

Kiteboarding Hot Spots

Kiteboarders need good equipment, and they also need a good place to practice. An ideal kiteboarding spot has perfect weather and water conditions. These are the best kiteboarding spots around the world:

1. Cabarete, Dominican Republic: The largest kiteboarding competition happens here each year.

2. Maui, Hawaii: This is a favorite kiteboarding spot. It is sunny and windy all year, and has monster waves in winter.

3. Tarifa, Spain: In a wind tunnel between the European and African continents, this is perfect for kiteboarders.

4. Cape Town, South Africa: The ocean off this large city has big swells and good wind.

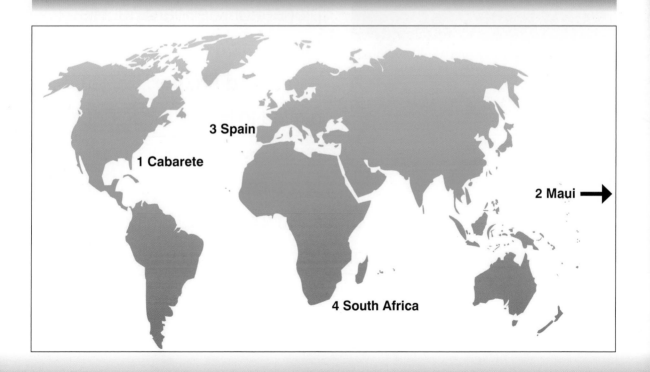

THE STARS

Few riders have been more important to the sport than Robby Naish.

Big air, awesome flight, and crazy tricks are expected in professional kiteboarding. Here are some of the biggest stars in the world.

ROBBY NAISH: KITEBOARDING PIONEER

Robby Naish is known as the pioneer of kiteboarding. His father was a competitive surfer and **board shaper**. His family moved to Hawaii when Robby was 11 years old. Soon, Robby began competing in the new sport of windsurfing. In the 1990s, Robby started kiteboarding, too. Since then he has won many world titles in windsurfing and kiteboarding. He also developed better equipment and exciting tricks for kiteboarding, such as kiteloops and megaloops.

RUBEN LENTEN: MASTER OF EXTREME

Ruben Lenten, from the Netherlands, loves pushing the limits. He wants to fly higher, go faster, and be more extreme! He has attended just about every kiteboarding competition for years, but he does not like the limitations put on kiteboarding. Now he is promoting extreme kiteboarding. This means doing risky **acrobatics** in storm conditions with powerful wind and huge waves.

Ruben Lenten is one of the best big-air riders.

SUSI MAI: AN INSPIRATION

Susi Mai is an inspiration to many in the kiteboarding world. Her passion is sharing kiteboarding with others. Susi works with KiteRight, a charity to improve kids' lives with kiting. She designs kiteboarding products for women to encourage more women to participate in the sport. Susi

Susi Mai is helping more people get into kiteboarding.

is also president and co-founder of MaiTai, an organization to help the environment. Susi was Queen of the Air three years in a row and placed in the top five for six years during the World Tour for the PKRA (Professional Kiteboard Riders Association).

AARON HADLOW: TRICK INVENTOR

Aaron Hadlow is from Great Britain, and he is one of the best kiteboarders in the world. Aaron has been competing since he was 14 years old and is known for creating new tricks. He has won the PKRA World Championships five times.

Even champions like Aaron Hadlow have to haul their kites in after a ride.

Gisela Pulido has been soaring over the kiteboarding world since she was just a kid.

GISELA PULIDO: YOUNGEST CHAMPION

Gisela Pulido is from Tarifa, Spain. In 2004, she became the youngest kiteboarding champion in the world at age 10! Growing up, she loved water sports, and she was a risk taker.

She swam competitively and snowboarded. Since her first big win, she has won championships in dozens of events. Her motto is: "Never give up!"

FASTER THAN THE WIND

Robbie Douglas and his brothers Morgan and Jamie are some of the fastest kiteboarders in the world. They go faster than a racing sailboat. They can ride at nearly 70 miles (112 kilometers) per hour—as fast as a car on the highway! A big **rooster tail** shoots up behind them as they ride that fast.

Robbie Douglas performs one of his record-setting speed runs.

High winds and great weather make the coast of Spain a kiteboarding hot spot.

The biggest kiteboarding events are the PKRA World Tour competitions. Each year the PKRA travels around the world. The athletes compete in places including France, Egypt, Brazil, Spain, Thailand, Germany, and the Dominican Republic. Riders compete in freestyle, big air, wave, and slalom. The best three results count toward the riders' global rank.

Another famous competition is the Red Bull King of the Air. This competition has been held in Maui, Hawaii, and Cape Town, South Africa. It pushes the limits for big-air kiters. The rules are simple—get the best, biggest, longest air. Kiters in this competition jump as high as 82 feet (25 meters) or as high as an eight-story building!

Many professional kiteboarders would like to see kiteboarding become an Olympic sport.

The Cape Doctor

In Cape Town, South Africa, the perfect kiteboarding conditions have a special name: the Cape Doctor. The Cape Doctor is a summer wind that can blow steadily at more than 34 miles (54 kilometers) per hour for training, competition, and fun.

Epic Moves

In 2011, professional kiter Ruben Lenten got big air to jump over a pier in Spain. He jumped from the Mediterranean Sea into the Atlantic Ocean!

There are many styles of kiteboarding. Freestyle, the most popular, is an anything goes style. Most boards today are designed for freestyling. Freestylers use the edges of their smaller boards to turn easily. Flat or choppy water is good for freestyling. Professional freestylers jump high into the air so they can do airborne tricks. This style is a popular competition event.

Wakestyle uses a wake-style board with **bindings** like a snowboard. Riders do tricks and jumps sometimes involving ramps, but they don't get as high as freestylers. Flat water is perfect for this style.

Wave riding is a cross between surfing and kiteboarding. Wave riders use a directional surfboard with a kite to pull them into position on big waves. Then the power of the wave takes over for them to surf.

Freestyle competitors flip, spin, and twist to score big points with judges.

TO VICTORY!

This is what *kiteboarding is all about!* Kevin Lagaree thought as he flew into the air. Climbing higher, he felt the rush. Kevin's kite pulled him almost 80 feet (24 meters) in the air! He loved that crazy sensation. Getting air is a fantastic feeling that all the riders love.

Before Kevin Lagaree takes to the air, he practices his speed moves.

Competing with 24 of the best kiteboarders in the world at the Red Bull King of the Air competition was like a dream. Kevin knew he was fighting for the title against the best riders like Ruben Lenten, Aaron Hadlow, and previous king Jesse Richman. They all wanted to push themselves and their sport to the limit.

Kevin is like a gymnast when he does acrobatics in midair.

Kevin rose into the sky. Once in the air he prepared to do a trick called a KGB. He was a little worried. A few years earlier, he had tried this trick at an event in Spain. When he landed, he hurt his knee. Would it happen again?

A bird? A plane? No, it's just Kevin soaring more than 70 feet (22 meters) in the air!

Now, in the beautiful aqua-blue water, Kevin tried a KGB again. He found the right place in the wind window for maximum speed. He eyed the perfect wave to launch from. His take off and rotation were perfect. He did a back flip, passed the handle bar around his back and did a full-circle, 360-degree spin. Then he stomped the landing! Perfect!

As Kevin came down from the sky in Cape Town, he knew he had done it. He landed the trick that once hurt him. A cheer went up from 10,000 spectators watching from the shore. The next day, Kevin Langeree proudly received the crown of Red Bull King of the Air!

Not every kiteboarding adventure ends up crowning a champion. But whether you ride for fun or for prizes, kiteboarding can surely take you places!

Kevin Langaree is crowned the highest-flying kiteboarder in the world in 2014.

GLOSSARY

acrobatics (AK-roh-BAT-iks): gymnastic moves done in the air while kiteboarding

aerial (AIR-ee-uhl): having to do with things in midair

bindings (BINE-dings): straps that hold a rider's feet to a wakeboard or windsurfing board

board shaper (BORED SHAPE-ur): a person who creates boards for water sports using tools and their hands

catamarans (KAT-uh-muh-ranz): sailing boats with two hulls, or bodies

gale-force (GALE-fors): a measurement of very high winds at 39 to 46 miles per hour (63 to 74 kilometers per hour)

GPS (JEE-PEE-ESS): initials for Global Positioning System, a collection of satellites that work with ground devices to locate a person on the Earth

harness (HARR-ness): a set of straps worn around the body that connects the kiteboarder to the control bar and the driving wires

intense (in-TENNS): calling for extreme effort or focus

knots (NOTS): a measurement of the speed of a boat on the water

rooster tail (ROO-ster TALE): a high, wide plume of water kicked up by a fast-moving watercraft

starboard (STAR-bird): in sailing terms, the direction otherwise known as right

whitecaps (WYTE-kaps): the wind-driven, white-colored tops of fast-moving ocean waves

wind window (WIND WIN-doh): the imaginary clock face that helps a kiteboarder choose which way to steer, using the wind at his or her back

INDEX

Cape Town 4, 39, 44

Cody, Samuel 11

Douglas, Robbie 39

Hadlow, Aaron 35, 43

kite-landboarding 17

Langaree, Kevin 4, 42, 43, 44, 45

Legaignoux, Dominique and
    Bruno 12, 14

Lenten, Ruben 33, 40, 43

Mai, Susie 34

Naish, Robby 32

PKRA World Championships 35, 39

Pulido, Gisela 38

Red Bull King of the Air 4, 39, 43, 45

Richman, Jesse 43

Roeseler, Cory 12, 14

wind window 19, 20, 21, 22

Wright, Orville and Wilbur 11

SHOW WHAT YOU KNOW

1. What is another name for the sport of kiteboarding?

2. How does a kiteboarder steer the kite?

3. What is the wind window?

4. Name three great places for kiteboarding.

5. What big title did Kevin Langeree win in 2014?

WEBSITES TO VISIT

www.prokitetour.com

www.inmotionkitesurfing.com/learn-to-kitesurf

www.actionsportsmaui.com/asmf_faq_kite.html

ABOUT THE AUTHOR

Betsy R. Cassriel is a faculty member and department chair at Santa Barbara City College. She has written three textbooks, including *Academic Connections 1* and *Stories Worth Reading 1 and 2* for learners of English as a second language. She has a BA in English from Westmont College and an MAT from the School for International Training in Vermont. She lives in Santa Barbara with her family, where kiteboarding is popular at the beach near her house!

Meet The Author!
www.meetREMauthors.com

www.rourkeeducationalmedia.com

PHOTO CREDITS: Cover © TKTKTKT
Interior: Dollar Photo: Intst 27; Dreamstime.com: Epicstock 6, 12; Adreleroux2 7; Netfalls 9; Dtfoxphoto 13; Frolovena 15; Chenchonghua 16; Pochiu 17; Aneese 18; Tan4ikk 19; Intst 21; Poco2005 22; Jdazuelos 25, title page; Nevenm 26; Jennyt 27; Scherbinator 28; Alexytrener 30; Etunya 31; Canaryluc 38. Adrien Freville: 37. Library of Congress: 10. Jordinkitelife.com: 43. Newscom: Nhat V. Meyer/KRT 33. Red Bull Content Pool: 32, 34, 35, 36, 42, 45. Shutterstock: Elena Frolova 23, 24, 41; withGod 29.

Edited by: Keli Sipperley
Produced by Shoreline Publishing Group
Design by: Bill Madrid, Madrid Design

Library of Congress PCN Data

Kiteboarding / Betsy R. Cassriel
 (Intense Sports)
  ISBN 978-1-63430-439-9 (hard cover)
  ISBN 978-1-63430-539-6 (soft cover)
  ISBN 978-1-63430-627-0 (e-Book)
Library of Congress Control Number: 2015932642
Printed in the United States of America, North Mankato, Minnesota

Also Available as:

ROURKE'S
e-Books